Also by Mary Rayner

Mr and Mrs Pig's Evening Out
Garth Pig and the Icecream Lady
Mrs Pig's Bulk Buy
One by One
Ten Pink Piglets
Mrs Pig Gets Cross

This edition first published in 1996 by
Macmillan Children's Books
a division of Macmillan Publishers Ltd,
25 Eccleston Place, London SW1W 9NF
and Basingstoke
Associated companies worldwide

ISBN 0 333 63751 8 (hardback)
ISBN 0 333 64499 9 (paperback)

Text and illustrations copyright © Mary Rayner 1986, 1996

1 3 5 7 9 8 6 4 2

A CIP catalogue record for this book is available from the British Library

Printed in Hong Kong

WICKED WILLIAM

Written and illustrated by
Mary Rayner

Macmillan Children's Books

Of all the ten piglets in the Pig family, William was the naughtiest. When he was small he had learnt to climb out of his cot earlier than any of the others, and as he grew bigger, when they all played games, it would be William who pretended to be the wicked one.

If Alun and Toby were policemen, William would be the bank robber, and if they all sat up the apple tree pretending it was a ship . . .

. . . William would be the one to climb
the highest swaying branch and tie on
a skull-and-crossbones flag and say
he was a pirate.

Some mornings William went down to breakfast while Mrs Pig was still dressing the two smallest piglets. She would come down to find all seven milk bottles with the cream neatly removed, and William halfway through his third bowl of cereal.

He could not resist teasing his two little brothers, Benjamin and Garth. Once, when all the piglets were tucked up for the night, William waited until Garth's eyes were closed and only the sound of him sucking his blanket showed that he wasn't quite asleep. Then William leaned over from his bunk and called down briskly, "Time to get up, Garth. It's morning time!"

And poor Garth had stumbled out of bed and gone
down to his mother and father saying, "It's not morning,
is it? William says it's morning."

"Oh, the devil!" Mrs Pig smiled in spite of herself as she
kissed Garth better and carried him upstairs again.

One morning William felt extra full of energy. He had
been away from school unwell, but was now quite better.
He had tied a hanky over his snout, and was pretending
to be a burglar.

"Can we play?" asked Benjamin and Garth.

"Oh, all right," said William.

"Wait for me," said Garth, and he ran off to the bathroom.

"D'you want help?" asked William.

"No. I can go all by myself," Garth called back.

Meanwhile William was stacking pieces of paper on the top bunk. "This will be the money I steal," he said to Ben, "and the bunk beds can be the house. I shall climb in and tie you and Garth up, and leave you in the top attic while I escape. It will take all day for anyone to find you."

Had it been such a good idea to ask to join in? Ben stood hesitating, but just then a terrible squealing came from the bathroom.

William and Benjamin ran towards the sound.

It was Garth, crying and beating on the door. "I can't get out. I can't open it. It's locked."

Mother Pig came hurrying up from the kitchen, wiping her wet trotters on a tea towel. "Now what have you done to him?" she snapped at William as he and Benjamin stood by the door.

"Nothing," said William indignantly. "He's locked himself in."

"It's all right, Garth," Mrs Pig called. "We'll soon have you out."

The squealing stopped. They could hear a tap running.

"Turn the tap off," shouted Mrs Pig through the keyhole.

"I can't, it's stuck!" And Garth began to cry again.

Mrs Pig looked worried. "How will we ever get him out?" she whispered. "There's only one little window, and the water will soon be everywhere."

"I can try and climb up to the window," said William. "I'm sure I can. I'm not too big to fit through it."

"Oh, William, yes," said his mother, and they ran down to the back of the house.

Carefully William started to scale the upright drain-pipe that led down the back wall. Water was beginning to stream out of the overflow pipe from the bath down on to the concrete path. Garth's anxious face appeared at the little window.

"It's all right," shouted William, "I'm coming."

With a struggle he reached the point where a second pipe joined the main one. It sloped sideways up towards the bathroom. Slowly William inched his way along it. Mrs Pig covered her eyes.

But not for nothing had William so often played at burglars. Within minutes he had reached the little window.

"Out of the way, Garth," and he levered himself up on to the window sill.

The two watching pigs below saw him disappear into the bathroom. In no time the tap was off, the door was open again, and Garth was freed.

"You climbed just like a real burglar," said Garth admiringly.

William grinned behind his hanky.

"I'm sorry, Will," said their mother, bringing a bucket and mop to clear up all the water. "I thought you were teasing him again."

"When I grow up," said Garth, "I'm going to be a burglar."